EMILIO

Bradbury Press · *New York*

A HOME

by Nola Langner Malone

Bradbury Press

An Affiliate of Macmillan, Inc.

866 Third Avenue, New York, NY 10022

Collier Macmillan Canada, Inc.

Printed and bound in Japan

10   9   8   7   6   5   4   3   2   1

Library of Congress Cataloging-in-Publication Data

Malone, Nola Langner.

A home.

Summary: Molly does not feel comfortable in her new
house until she makes friends with a girl named Miranda
Marie.

[1. Moving, Household—Fiction.   2. Friendship—
Fiction] I. Title.

PZ7.M2966Ho 1988   [E]   87-17849

ISBN 0-02-751440-4

For Lisa Langner, my first daughter.
For Bruce Musicus, my new son.
For the Best Married Couple.
With my love.

One cold day in the middle of March,
Molly moved to a new big house.
Good-bye Rock.
Good-bye Pond.
And Good-bye Creaky Swing.

She took her silky blanket.
She took her backpack.
And walked slowly, very slowly to the car.

They arrived at the new big house.

Molly sat in her empty room.

Nothing looked right anymore.

The bed stuck out.

The ceiling leaned in.

Big cardboard boxes covered the floor.

Molly held her blanket tight.
"I will never move again," she said.

There was a knock at Molly's door.
"Come in," she said,
wishing they would go away.
In walked Miranda Marie.

"Hi!" she said.

"My name's Miranda Marie.
  I live next door.
  Let's be friends!"
Molly smiled for the first time since Sunday.

They played Pigs in the Mud.

Fish in the Water.

Caterpillars dancing.
Leaping up. Bouncing down.
Dancing side by side.

The sky got dark.
The stars came out.
They went outside
to make a wish.

"Star light, star bright," said Molly.

"First star I see tonight," said Miranda Marie.

"First star WHO sees tonight?" said Molly.

"ME!" said Miranda Marie.

"ME!" said Molly.

 And they had a fight.

They pinched and they poked.
They pushed and they shoved.
They landed on the cold wet ground.

Miranda Marie stood up.
She brushed herself off.
"So who cares?" she said.
And she walked away.
Molly stayed there for a while.
The sky was full of stars,
But it was too dark.
Too dark to be alone.
She missed Miranda Marie.

Molly walked slowly,
very slowly
back to her room
in the new big house.

She stood at the window.

She looked outside.

Miranda Marie's house was all lit up.

It was so close that Molly could almost touch it.

Miranda Marie was in her room.

Molly opened her window.

Miranda Marie opened hers.

"Hi," said Molly. "I was looking for you."

"Me, too," said Miranda Marie.

"Guess what?" said Molly. "I missed you."

"Me, too," said Miranda Marie.

"See you in the morning," Molly called to Miranda Marie.

"In the morning," Miranda Marie called back.

Molly took her silky blanket and got into bed.

Her new room looked good in the night.
Stars at the window.
Friendly shadows on the wall.
Silky blanket by her head.
Molly was home.